Why Chri
San

Writt

RON ROECKER

Also Available on Amazon Worldwide:

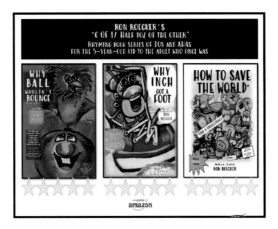

Why Ball Wouldn't Bounce
*Named to "Best Children's Books of All-Time" and
"Best New Children's Books to Read in 2020" Lists
by BookAuthority.org*

Why Inch Got a Foot
"Endearing from the very first page with a totally adorable
new character in 'Inch.'" Prairies Book Review

How to Save the World: Find a Smallisall

-Amazon

Paperback and eBook Kindle Editions Available.

Dedicated to...

My family, on Earth and in Heaven,
who always made Christmas the
most wonderful time of the year.

WHY CHRISTMAS IS CANCELLED

Santa Spells it Out

Written & Illustrated by
RON ROECKER

Author of
"Why Ball Wouldn't Bounce"
"Why Inch Got a Foot"

★★★★★
-Amazon

'Twas the night before Christmas
When all through my shop,
Not a creature was stirring
for all work had stopped.

Mrs. Claus with Sudoku
and I on the couch…
How did this happen?
Let me spell it out!

There once was a time
I made such a clatter
When naughty was bad
and nice seemed to matter;

When children wrote letters
to me once a year
(a letter is something you write…
starts with 'Dear…')

With every "I" dotted
and every "T" crossed,
The first letters came
Before there was frost.
I'd read every list
Three times to the end…
(They believed in the magic
and I in them.)

Ev'ry request was time-stamped and filed,
Each coded and noted for every child.
Then on to the "BIG" Lists,
Which, of course, were checked twice!
(Back then, maybe once 'cause
most folks *were* "NICE.")

NICE

For so many children
and grown-ups would write
About those in need
or pure souls full of light,
Intending to donate
what they would receive,
To angels beside us
So all would believe.

Yes, "Do Unto Others"
& "love those next door"
Were practiced and preached
by the rich and the poor.
I always received
a mountain of mail,
From all 'round the globe,
each year, without fail.

(Let it out, Papa…)

Our written connection
would soon start to fade,
As high-tech connections
became all the rage.
It started with dial-up
and emails appeared,
The elves told me,
"Santa, there's nothing to fear!"

Then, oh, Bah Humbug!
I.M. was the tech!
BLIP "What's Up?" *BLIP*
'What's that blip, what the heck?!!'

Then buh-bye I.M.s
as texts soon came raging,
Ending all phone calls
and who recalls paging?!

More rapid than eagles
the platforms all came.
You friended and posted
and tagged them by name:

On Friendster, on MySpace,
then Facebook and Twitter
On Tumblr, on YouTube,
on Snapchat with glitter.

On Insta, on Tik Tok
on LikedIn, but why?!
"Which iPhone is next,
what else must I buy?"

With every connection
you grew out of touch.
Coffee dates? Game nights?
No more, not so much!

Then nobody cared
about naughty or nice
You might be upgraded;
I ask at what price?

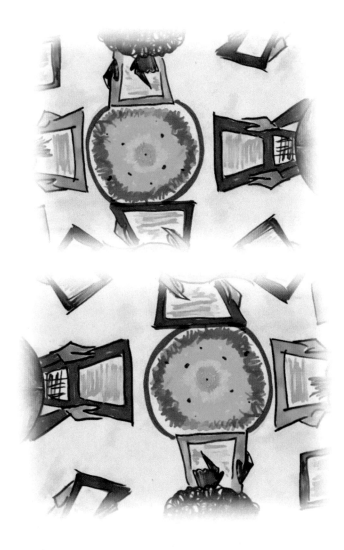

Then sentences shunned
and real words dismissed.
You typed "BTW"
and grammar was dissed.
And what to my wondering
eyes should appear?
Our mailman with NOTHING!
No, nada, all year!!

No letters? No wonder?
No kids on my knee?
I've had it! I'm Santa.
Please listen to me!

Without any letters or wishes to fill,
The elves have no reason
to sing or to build...

And reindeer won't fly
if there's nothing to haul,
So I Zoomed and said,
"dash away, dash away all!"

Yes, Christmas is cancelled
But don't sit and mope.
We'll live without gifts,
But not without hope!

So, I've written this text
to remind you how good,
Using a sentence
can be and you should,
Remember what's better
(I know you can tell),
Laughing out loud
or typing CAPS LOL?

Real human connection
we all need to find,
And the child inside
for the good of All-Kind.

It's time to look up
and put tech in its place.
Let's talk with each other,
offline, face-to-face.

There might be some hope
to save Christmas day.
If everyone does
Whatever I say.
No chaos, no stress outs,
no tensions that mount;
It's being together,
connecting that counts.

Talk about Christmas
when Grandma was small,
Then ask Aunts and Uncles
their best gifts of all;
Start new traditions,
adopt a new cause.
For more great ideas,
Search "Ask Mrs. Claus."

If we do our part
to unplug and connect,
And promise to live
with more kindness, respect
--nothing we need is
online or in malls--
Then Christmas might happen
this year after all!

Now, before I end
this global group text,
And lives get consumed
with what now and next,
You really should know
(I checked them both twice)
You're real close to "Naughty"
(but inching toward "Nice.")

What else, Mrs. Claus,
What did I forget?

"Sweet Santa,
please tell them.
Your wish is legit!"

My one final wish
for the world on this night
is Merry Christmas to All
and to All…

por favor escribe
bitte schreibe
s'il vous plait écrivez
per favore scrivi
por favor, escreva
kérlek írj

書いてください

tafadhali andika

Schrijf alsjeblieft

e ʻoluʻolu e kākau

لـطفـا بـنـويـسيـد
Skriv venligst
Παρακαλώ γράψτε
ביטע שרייב

tanpri ekri
scríobh le do thoil

Please Write.

(The End)

Follow Ron on Amazon and his "Lightly Seasoned" Series
on Facebook:
www.facebook.com/ronwroteit

Also available by Ron Roecker:

"6 of 1/ Half Doz of the Other"
Rhyming Book Series of DOs and AHAs for the
<u>5-Year-Old Kid to the Adult Who Once Was</u>

Book 1: "Why Ball Wouldn't Bounce"
Book 2: "Why Inch Got a Foot"
Book 3: "How to Save the World: Find a Smallisall"

available at
amazon

Made in the USA
Columbia, SC
23 October 2020